THERE ONCE WAS A COWPOKE WHO SWALLOWED AN ANT

HELEN KETTEMAN

Illustrated by WILL TERRY

www.av2books.com

First Published by

ALBERT WHITMAN & COMPANY
Publishing children's books since 1919

There once was a cowpoke who swallowed an ant—
a fiery thing with a Texas-sized sting.

The cowpoke panted, and his voice got higher.

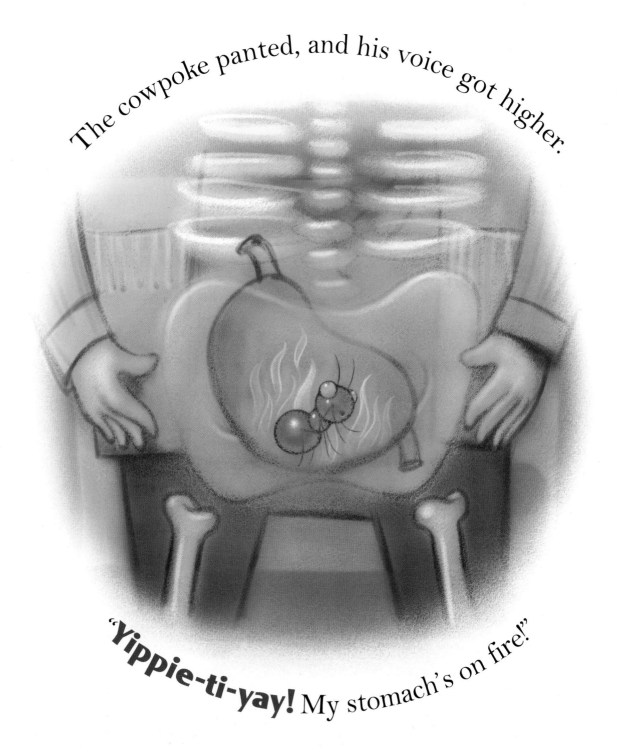

'Yippie-ti-yay! My stomach's on fire!'

So he swallowed a spider, leggy and hairy,
That was big as a bat and horribly scary.

He swallowed the spider
to bite the ant
that was stinging his stomach and making him pant.

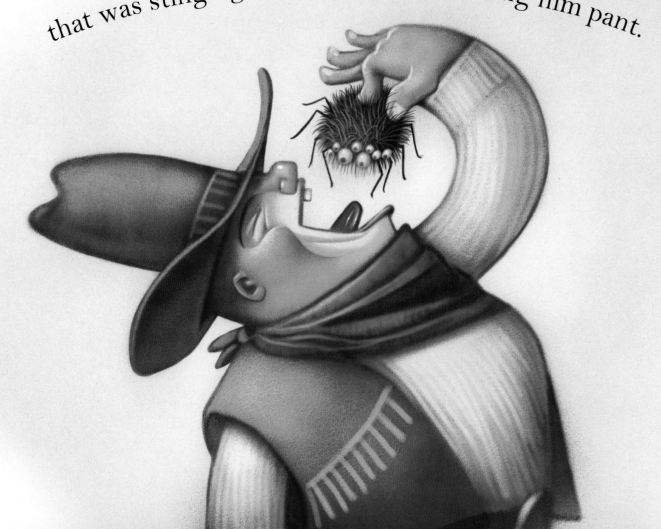

4

But Spider's legs **wiggled** and **waggled**,  and the cowpoke's stomach **jiggled** and **jaggled**.

So he swallowed a roadrunner, hungry and lean,
to dash right in and clean up the scene.

6

He swallowed Roadrunner
to eat the spider
to bite the ant
that was stinging his stomach
and making him pant.

But Roadrunner ran so lightning quick
that Cowpoke started to get seasick.

7

So he swallowed a lizard, a horned, spiky critter that was scratchy to swallow and terribly bitter.

He swallowed the lizard
to chase Roadrunner
to eat the spider
to bite the ant

that was stinging his stomach
and making him pant.

But Lizard's skin was **scratchity-scritchy** and the cowpoke's stomach got terribly itchy.

So he swallowed a 'dillo, the nine-banded type, that was hard as a rock and smelled really ripe.

11

He swallowed the 'dillo
to scare the lizard
to chase Roadrunner
to eat the spider
to bite the ant
that was stinging his stomach
and making him pant.

But 'dillo's claws were sharp as a pointy old rake,
so the cowpoke rustled a rattle-tailed snake.

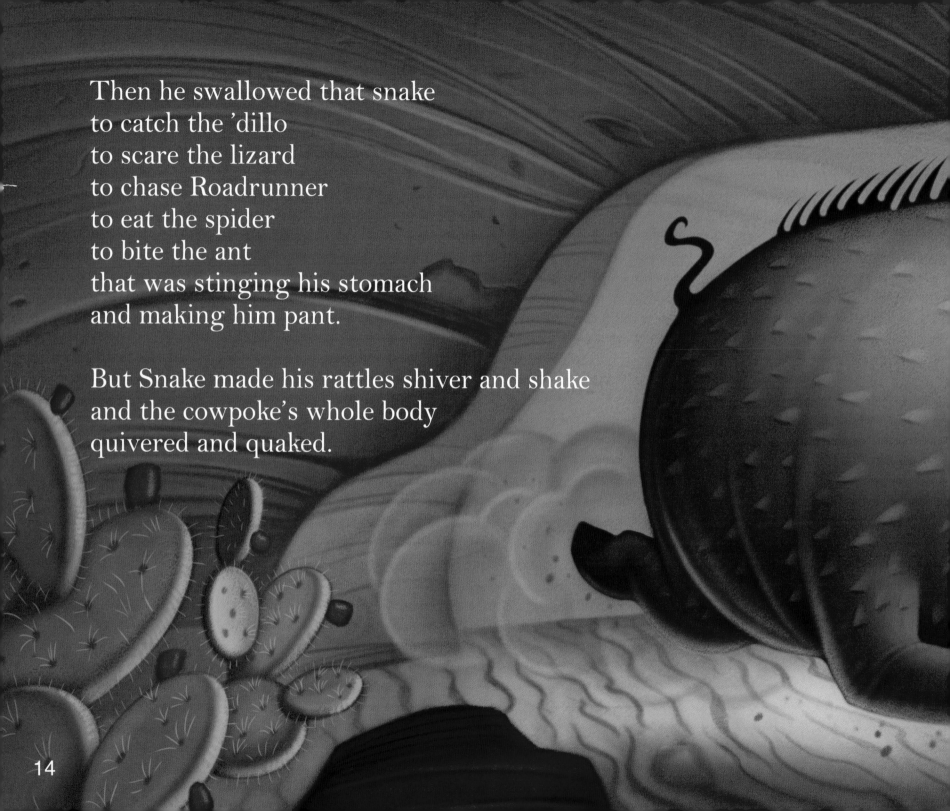

Then he swallowed that snake
to catch the 'dillo
to scare the lizard
to chase Roadrunner
to eat the spider
to bite the ant
that was stinging his stomach
and making him pant.

But Snake made his rattles shiver and shake
and the cowpoke's whole body
quivered and quaked.

So he swallowed a boar, nasty and mean,
with the sharpest tusks he'd ever seen

But Boar's tusks jabbed the cowpoke instead,
and the cowpoke shouted, "I wish I wuz dead!"

He swallowed the boar

to poke the snake

to catch the 'dillo

to scare the lizard

to chase Roadrunner

to eat the spider

to bite the ant

that was stinging his stomach

and making him pant.

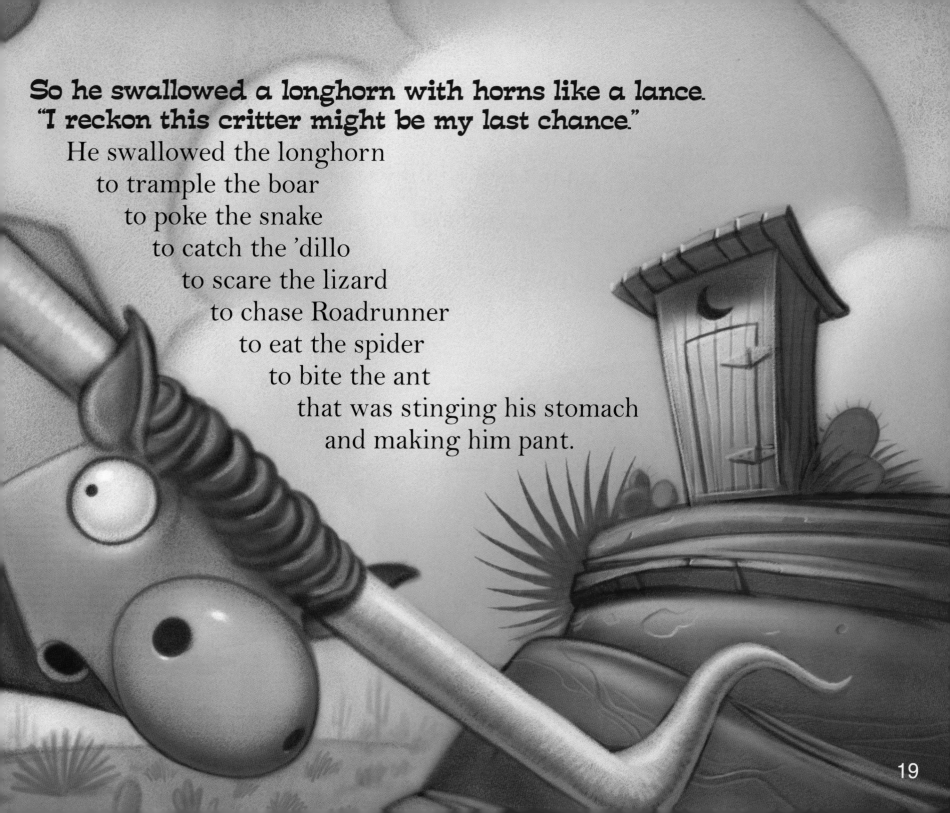

So he swallowed a longhorn with horns like a lance.
"I reckon this critter might be my last chance."
He swallowed the longhorn
to trample the boar
to poke the snake
to catch the 'dillo
to scare the lizard
to chase Roadrunner
to eat the spider
to bite the ant
that was stinging his stomach
and making him pant.

19

When Longhorn showed up, Boar set off like a flash.
Longhorn couldn't catch him to turn him to mash.
The cowpoke got mad and stomped on his hat.
"I'll just do it myself! I reckon that's that."

Then he saddled his horse, took his rope off the shelf.
"If I want it done right, I'll do it myself."

So he swallowed his rope,
he swallowed his horse,
and then he swallowed
himself, of course.

He swallowed himself
to lasso the longhorn
to trample the boar
to poke the snake
to catch the 'dillo
to scare the lizard
to chase Roadrunner
to eat the spider
to bite the ant
that was stinging his stomach
and making him pant.

24

He jumped on his horse
and rode with great speed
and lassoed the longhorn
to start the stampede.

AND FINALLY...

OUT raced Longhorn with the lasso a-flappin',

OUT followed Boar, his hooves just a-tappin',

OUT slithered Snake, in a very fast crawl,

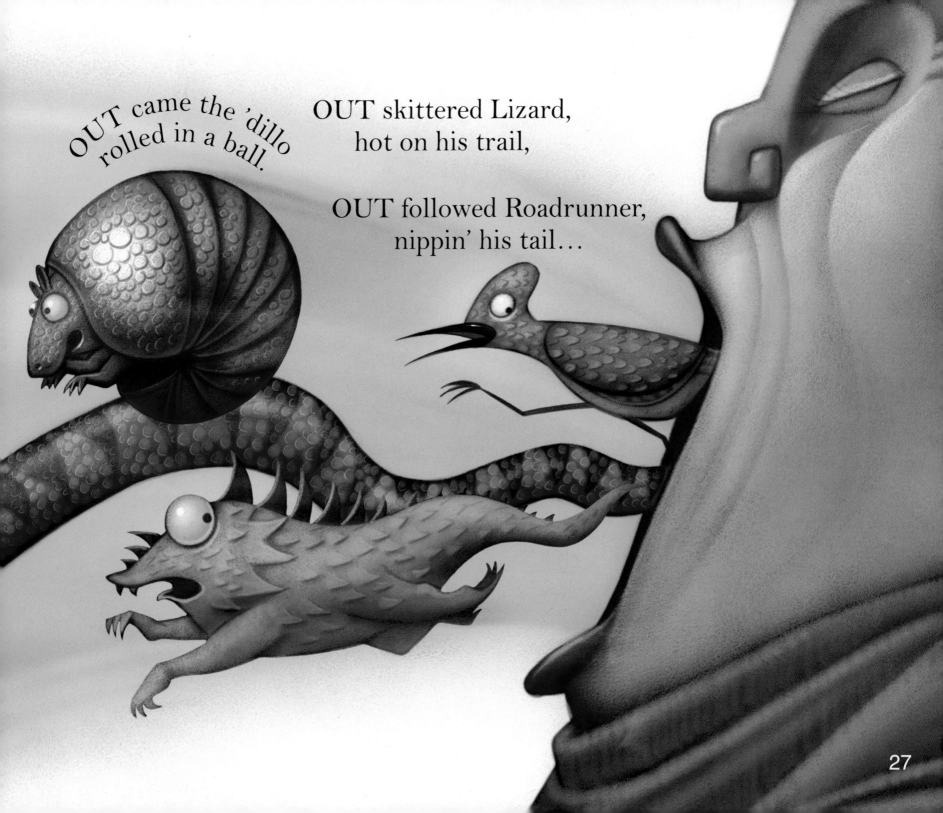

OUT came the 'dillo
rolled in a ball.

OUT skittered Lizard,
hot on his trail,

OUT followed Roadrunner,
nippin' his tail…

27

OUT raced Spider,
jack-rabbit fast.

And then came the ant,
rid of **AT LAST**.

The cowpoke climbed off his horse.
"Whew! I'm all spent.
My get up and go has got up and went."

30

So he pulled his boots off his feet
and his hat off his head.

Then he shuffled inside and fell into bed.

Your AV² Media Enhanced book gives you a fiction readalong online.
Log on to www.av2books.com and enter the unique book code from
page 2 to use your readalong.

AV² Readalong Navigation

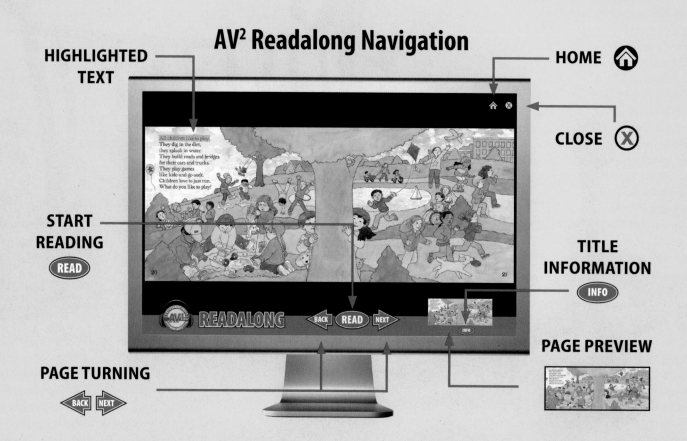

HIGHLIGHTED
TEXT

HOME

CLOSE

START
READING

READ

TITLE
INFORMATION

INFO

PAGE TURNING

PAGE PREVIEW

Published by AV² by Weigl
350 5ᵗʰ Avenue, 59ᵗʰ Floor New York, NY 10118
Websites: www.av2books.com   www.weigl.com

Printed in the United States of America in North Mankato, Minnesota
1 2 3 4 5 6 7 8 9 0 18 17 16 15 14

042014
WEP080414

Library of Congress Control Number: 2014937834

ISBN 978-1-4896-2383-6 (hardcover)
ISBN 978-1-4896-2384-3 (single user eBook)
ISBN 978-1-4896-2385-0 (multi-user eBook)

Text copyright © 2014 by Helen Ketteman.
Illustrations copyright © 2014 by Will Terry.
Published in 2014 by Albert Whitman & Company.